The Plug at the Bottom of the Sea

"Hold tight me hearties!" shouted Aunt Tabitha with excitement, for the current was sucking the bathysphere down the plug hole and the Lantern Fish were dashing for cover in their homes among the rocks.

"Stand by for more adventure!" she called, waving a packet of chocolate biscuits above the din. With incredible speed the bathysphere shot into the opening and down the tunnel.

Brice Avery

The Plug at the Bottom of the Sea

Illustrated by John Eastwood

Hippo

For the Thomson family –
Ali, Mags, Jon, David and Peter.

Scholastic Children's Books,
Commonwealth House, 1-19 New Oxford Street,
London WC1A 1NU, UK
a division of Scholastic Ltd
London ~ New York ~ Toronto ~ Sydney ~ Auckland

Published in the UK by Scholastic Ltd, 1997

Text copyright © Brice Avery, 1997
Illustrations copyright © John Eastwood, 1997

ISBN 0 590 19108 X

Printed by Cox & Wyman Ltd, Reading, Berks

1 3 5 7 9 10 8 6 4 2

Chapter 1

The problem with being a fish, thought Timothy Thompson as he slid out of bed and on to the floor with a thud, is that it takes so long to get down to breakfast. He rolled and wiggled out of his room and on to the landing. "When I rule the world," he said out loud, "I'm going to make a law that says that all fish can opt for breakfast in bed if they don't fancy swimming on the carpet." With that, he launched himself sliding and grunting down the stairs, and ended up in a tangled mess at the bottom.

His mother and father, alerted by the strange noises, peered from the kitchen doorway and watched as Timothy wrestled with a luminous tennis-ball on the end of a piece of stiff wire attached to a head-band.

"What are you doing?" his mother enquired.

"Straightening my lantern so I can lure some breakfast into my mouth," he replied, gnashing his teeth and waving the luminous tennis-ball around on the end of the coat-hanger.

"But it's only a tennis-ball."

"To you it's a tennis-ball – to me it's the difference between survival and starvation," he replied grandly. "After all, without my friendly lure to guide them, how will the little fish know where to come to get eaten?"

Timothy's parents, who were both scientists, had to go to a very important conference. With other scientists they were trying to stop the oceans rising and the rivers drying up – a problem that was affecting crops and seaside towns. The crops weren't growing and the towns that had been inland were now by the sea and the towns that were by the sea were now under water, which was inconvenient for shopping. The other problem was that there was less room for people to build

houses and have farms, so something had to be done. Timothy had offered to help and suggested that the answer might be at the bottom of the sea. But nobody listened to him because they thought he was just a kid with a tennis-ball on his head.

"I hope you are going to behave a little better than this for your new uncle," said his father, trying to sound cross. "He might not be as understanding as we are."

"I don't call taking my lantern away when I'm trying to eat deep-sea crustaceans understanding."

"And I don't call whacking a tennis-ball up and down in your cornflakes good behaviour."

While Timothy was trying to lure some crustaceans into his mouth,

a strange van drew up at the end of his street. It was the size of a removal lorry, painted black all over and driven by an odd-looking woman with a man sitting next to her. She had a determined but kind-looking face, earrings the size of dinner plates and was dressed from head to toe in black. Apart from that, she

blended in very well with the quiet, leafy well-to-do surroundings. The man jumped down from the cab, buttoned up a long and rather plain coat, pulled on a particularly dull-looking cap and, stuffing his long silvery hair into it, strode off towards Timothy's house.

He rang the doorbell.

"That will be your new uncle come to look after you while we are away," said Timothy's father.

"Great. Forced to be good by a total stranger while you go off to a party somewhere."

"It's not a party and he's not a stranger," Timothy's mother explained. "He's called Uncle Peregrine and he was recommended by the Uncle Agency as good with problem cases."

The truth was that Timothy's parents were really very clever scientists and often had to go away to important conferences. Unfortunately Timothy had exhausted the supply of relatives, nannies, babysitters and foster grannies to look after him. Most had resigned;

some had fled the country; and a good number, despite the very best medical help, were still recovering in quiet nursing homes in the country. The

ring at the door was the Thompsons' last hope so they went and answered it.

Uncle Peregrine was a bit older than Timothy's father and looked, at first sight, rather boring; but Timothy could see, with the eye of a seasoned professional, that this was no ordinary uncle. For one thing, he refused to take his coat off even though it was summer; and for another there was a piece of strange-coloured cloth hanging down from the end of his sleeve. Clearly this uncle had secrets – and secrets meant fun.

Chapter 2

Soon Timothy's parents disappeared down the road to their conference, a little doubtful in their minds about things. They were in such a hurry that they didn't even notice the black van and its strange driver waiting outside the house.

Uncle Peregrine pulled off his cap and

coat and threw them into the bin.

"That's better," he said, taking a swig of jungle juice from a leather bottle and handing it to Timothy to try. He wore a brightly-coloured jacket made of many different patches all sewn together higgledy-piggledy. His shirt was bright green and so were his trousers.

Little things on bits of string hung down from his jacket and stuck out of his pockets – a large spanner, a wooden spoon, bones, skulls of small beasts, tiny dark blue bottles and sundry leather pouches. In fact all the sort of things that a proper thorough-going copper-bottomed gold-plated uncle ought to have and so few seem to these days.

"Right, what do you want to do?" asked Uncle Peregrine simply.

"Go and see the Lantern Fish at the bottom of the sea," responded Timothy, who knew that the only way to test a grown-up properly was to the absolute limits.

"Okay, let's go," said Uncle Peregrine and turned for the door.

Timothy just had time to grab his tennis-ball and coat-hanger before locking the house and running after his new and, he hoped, extremely rewarding Uncle Peregrine.

The woman in the van introduced herself as Aunt Tabitha, shook his hand, tousled his hair and generally did all the things that an aunt should do but not, as is so often the case with aunts, to excess.

With an operatic twist she started the engine.

"To the sea," she announced.

"Tell us about Lantern Fish, Timothy Scientist," instructed Uncle Peregrine as they rumbled through the lanes towards the coast.

"Well, they live at the bottom of the sea where there is no light at all from the sun and where it is very cold and creepy and quiet. They have huge mouths, eat sea cucumbers and hunt in packs."

"Mmmm, sounds like my sort of thing," said Aunt Tabitha happily as she swung the van deftly on to the sand at the top of a crowded beach. "Tell me more."

"Well, they have a little lantern on the end of a thing that pokes out over the top of their head, like this," Timothy said, nodding his tennis-ball. "It lures crabs and small fish to their doom."

Aunt Tabitha let go of the wheel, smacked her ring-encrusted hands together and rubbed them with glee.

"Looks like a proper test for the Self-Propelled Deep-Sea Bathysphere," she announced, her eyes shining.

A bossy-looking deck-chair attendant came up and banged on the window of the van. Aunt Tabitha, who always took any opportunity to make a new friend, grinned and pressed her face against the glass.

The attendant, who always took any opportunity to make a new enemy, pressed his face against the glass and shouted, "You can't park that thing here!"

"Just have, old boy," she told him in a deck-chair attendant deflating kind of voice and he shuffled off to have a nice lie-down.

Chapter 3

Together they unloaded their home-made bathysphere from the back of the van and wheeled it down to the water's edge. People on the beach were so amazed by what was happening that they just stood and stared open-mouthed.

The bathysphere was bright green with yellow stripes and round like an orange – there was a lid and an observation bubble on the top, windows all over it and propellers, batteries, hydraulic arms, scoops and spotlights bolted on the sides.

Taking a large picnic hamper they climbed in at the top and shut the lid behind them. Timothy looked out through one of the windows. People were standing back and pointing.

"Engage forward thrust, dearest," said Uncle Peregrine.

"Engaging forward thrust."

"Brakes off please, Timothy."

Timothy grabbed the handle marked "GRAB" and pushed. "Brakes off, Uncle," he replied happily. The bathysphere lurched forward across the remaining few metres of the sand and into the waves.

To start with they stayed on the surface and motored along with the nose of the bathysphere pushing its way through the sunlit waves.

Timothy stuck his head into the observation bubble in the very top of the cabin and looked backwards.

"The beach seems a long way off already," he announced from his look-out point. "Everyone is standing and watching. Everyone that is except the deck-chair attendant."

Aunt Tabitha pushed her head up beside Timothy and together they watched as the now distant figure nosed around the van and looked into the open doors at the back.

"We forgot to close the van doors," she called down to Uncle Peregrine who was at the controls.

Without taking his eyes off the sea in front of him, Uncle Peregrine rummaged through the pockets of his patchwork jacket but he didn't find what he was looking for. Next he reached into what would have been the glove compartment of the bathysphere if he or Aunt Tabitha had ever owned a pair of gloves. It was full of small but indispensable items such as corkscrews, spare fuses and pictures of rare and poisonous toadstools.

Eventually he found a little box – about the size of a pencil-case – and handed it up to the others.

Aunt Tabitha extended a long silver aerial which was sticking out of the top and pushed a big red button on the front.

"Let's hope we are still in range," she said as they squinted to make out what was happening on the beach.

The nosy deck-chair attendant had by now plucked up the courage to climb into the back of the van and start fiddling with things that weren't his to fiddle with. He noticed too late that the radio signal from the bathysphere had started the automatic door-closing mechanism.

People on the beach watched with satisfaction as the panic-stricken deck-chair attendant disappeared behind the big metal doors. All that was left sticking out was the highly-polished peak of his municipal peaked cap.

"Free deck-chairs and no beach rules until we get back and release him," chuckled Aunt Tabitha.

"How long will that be?"

"Who knows," she replied, descending from the bubble with an elegant wave of her ring-encrusted hand. "Don't worry, there's half a dozen emergency hampers in the van – he won't go hungry."

Timothy grinned to himself and at the same moment Uncle Peregrine let water into the buoyancy tanks so that the bathysphere dived. Cold green water

washed over the bubble, right next to Timothy's head.

They followed the sandy bottom as it slanted slowly deeper and deeper out to sea. There was enough light filtering down from above for them to see where they were going through the porthole at the front. Every now and then the sand ahead of them would explode as a giant halibut or manta ray, which thought it was well hidden, changed its mind.

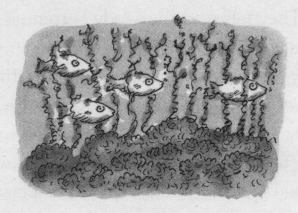

Chapter 4

Bit by bit the sand disappeared under a dense forest of brown, green and red seaweed. The uppermost fronds and branches stroked the bathysphere as it slid through the forest canopy. Every now and then they disturbed brightly-coloured fish which fed and nested in the seaweed. Once they even had to veer the bathysphere quickly to avoid a stampede of tiny but determined sea horses that were coming straight at them.

"The forest has stopped. It's a sort of stubby sea grass now," explained Timothy who was looking down through the bubble in the bottom of the bathysphere.

Suddenly all around the bathysphere were hundreds of silver streaks swimming this way and that at great speed.

"Sardines. Yum yum," said Aunt Tabitha, licking her lips noisily.

The three explorers watched as the little fish darted about, grazing on the sea grass and pretending that they weren't afraid of being eaten by bigger fish. They all swam in one direction and then, as if following some dance of their own, suddenly swerved, each one at the same time, and swam in another direction.

"I hope they don't foul the propellers," said Uncle Peregrine. "They aren't big enough to get out of the way." With that he shut down the engines and they settled on to the bottom to wait until the sardine shoal moved away.

Aunt Tabitha pulled the wicker basket
on to her lap, unfastened the buckles and
folded back the lid, which made an
encouraging creak. "Picnic time," she
announced. "Sandwich, anyone?"

Timothy found that all the excitement
had made him quite peckish. "What
flavours are there?" he enquired.

"Fish paste or cheese and chutney."

The idea of fish paste made Timothy feel a bit queasy so he opted for a cheese sandwich.

Uncle Peregrine handed him the leather bottle of jungle juice to wash it down with. "I don't know why, but I can't see the seabed in front of us," he said, running his fingers along the rows of switches on the control panel. "I'll turn on the spotlights."

With a loud click the spotlights came on and shone through the water like sunbeams through smoke.

"The seabed has disappeared!" exclaimed Timothy, pointing to where the beams of the spotlights shone down ahead of them into nothing but inky blackness. "We must have stopped on the very edge of the continental shelf."

They all peered in silence at the nothingness ahead and felt a little frightened. Timothy wondered if they would ever get to the bottom of the sea and if they did whether or not the Lantern Fish would be there.

"Never fear, me hearties," sang Aunt Tabitha, rattling her rings for good luck. Uncle Peregrine swung a marsupial skull round his head on a piece of string so that its teeth chattered in the breeze.

He said it was for good luck as well but Timothy reckoned he did it just to be shocking which is, after all, a much better reason for swinging bones round one's head.

Aunt Tabitha stared at them, her eyes shining with excitement. "Anything we find down there will probably be more frightened of us than we are of it," she declared emphatically.

Looking at her as she jangled her jewels, Timothy was inclined to agree. My new Aunt Tabitha is definitely the most terrifying thing I have ever seen, he thought to himself with satisfaction.

Can YOU read four Young Hippo books?

YOUNG HIPPO Readometer

The Young Hippo is sending a special prize to everyone who collects any four of these stickers, which can be found in Young Hippo books.

This is one sticker to stick on your own Young Hippo Readometer Card!

Collect four stickers and fill up your Readometer Card

There are all these stickers to collect too!

Get your Young Hippo Readometer Card from your local bookshop, or by sending your name and address to:

Chapter 5

Uncle Peregrine let off the brake, revved the motors and sent them shooting out over the edge of the continental shelf. He emptied the remaining buoyancy tanks, and the bathysphere with its three explorers on board dropped into the cold dark unknown.

Eventually they found the bottom

again, except that this time instead of sloping gently it was very steep. Steering the bathysphere was like half running and half falling down a very steep rocky hill.

"What's that?" exclaimed Aunt Tabitha, pointing out of the starboard porthole.

Timothy, who was now sitting in the spare seat at the control panel, moved a little lever, and outside one of the spotlights swivelled its beam on to an enormous grey fish with a big gaping mouth and eyes that shone back in the beam of light.

"I think it's a cod fish," he said,
consulting his battered and well
thumbed copy of *The Observer's Guide to
Denizens of the Deep.*

"He's a mean-looking customer,"
observed his aunt, wrapping her long
black scarf round her neck a few more
times for security. She pushed her face up
against the porthole and rattled her
earrings.

The cod fish, which had until then just been cruising along gently beside them, suddenly took fright and darted off into the night.

"Ha!" said Aunt Tabitha triumphantly. "He didn't like my jewels. There's one cod fish that knows when he's totally out-classed."

Down and down they went.

Timothy looked at the depth gauge.

"We are now in the region where only monsters and denizens of the deep live," he announced, peering through the window with pleasure.

Deeper and deeper they sank until the instruments showed that, finally, they were approaching the very bottom of the deepest part of the ocean.

Uncle Peregrine adjusted the speed of descent and brought the craft to rest with a tiny but very satisfying metallic clunk. With all the lights turned off they strained their eyes hopefully into the darkness.

"Can't see any jolly old Lantern Fish," said Aunt Tabitha, rummaging for her jar of pickled onions.

Timothy adjusted his coat-hanger and pushed his nose against the glass of the observation bubble. The blackness and gloom began at the end of his nose and seemed to go on for ever.

Timothy sighed and wondered if he would ever see a real Lantern Fish.

Suddenly a little greeny-yellow light turned on and he was looking straight into the face of a Lantern Fish.

"There is one looking at me through the window," he whispered, in case he scared it. He bobbed his luminous tennis-ball up and down and opened and closed his mouth. The Lantern Fish did the same a couple of times and then, flashing its light in a friendly way, carefully led the bathysphere on a secret journey across the seabed.

Chapter 6

Soon in the blackness ahead they saw a much larger glow of light.

"It's hundreds of Lantern Fish," exclaimed Uncle Peregrine, skilfully manoeuvring the craft nearer.

"More like thousands," corrected Timothy.

Indeed, thousands of Lantern Fish

were all around them. They were all holding on to long ropes of seaweed with their mouths and flashing their lanterns on and off. Together they looked like giant strings of Christmas-tree lights, each one contributing to the eerie glow.

"What are they pulling at?" asked Timothy out loud. For the fish were all

straining their fins in one direction, heaving on the seaweed ropes.

Timothy took the controls, followed the ropes to where they all met, and found that they were attached to an enormous stone plug embedded in the floor of the sea.

Their little Lantern Fish guide swam off to join the others and left Uncle Peregrine, Aunt Tabitha and Timothy to stare in wonder. Scattered all over and around the plug were piles and piles of junk. There were large things like bits of boat, a propeller, a gun, a capstan, bits of mast and even the metal dragon's head from a Phoenician slave galley. There were smaller things like clay jars, plastic toys and canisters of toxic waste as well.

"Look, there's a shopping trolley and a pram and an old boot over there," said Timothy, pointing out of the observation bubble. "Surely they weren't heaved over the side of a boat."

"More likely washed downstream from some distant river," replied his uncle sadly.

Timothy thought hard. "It must be the Lantern Fishes' job to let some water out now and then so that it flows into the middle of the earth and back out of the mountains," he worked out like the good scientist that he was.

Between them they decided that the plug which the Lantern Fish were trying to pull out was the reason that the oceans were rising and the rivers were drying up.

"And all that rubbish is making it impossible to shift," observed his Aunt Tabitha, who was feeling better after a couple of cucumber sandwiches with the crusts cut off. Uncle Peregrine's contribution was to punch some of the more interesting-looking buttons on the instrument panel, jerk a couple of chrome-plated levers, place one finger on an insignificant-looking toothed wheel and, with a practised flourish, give it an experimental tweak. The robotic arms on the front of the craft came instantly to life.

"Full ahead motors," he ordered.

"Full ahead aye," responded Timothy, and with tiny movements of the control stick he steered the craft up to the first piece of rubbish. There was a pleasing scrunch of cheap metal as the robotic arms closed on the handle of the shopping trolley.

"Reverse motors," instructed Uncle Peregrine and they dragged the trolley away and dropped it into a volcanic crevasse which Aunt Tabitha, using her artistic temperament, had selected for the purpose. With their wide eyes, big mouths and see-through bodies the Lantern Fish looked on, flashing their lanterns with approval.

After several hours of straining its motors, pushing and dragging all the bits of wood and metal and plastic, the tiny home-made bathysphere cleared all the rubbish off the plug and popped it down a succession of convenient crevasses. At the bottom of each crevasse the rubbish was melted down and, as the newly-formed rocks cooled, it showed up as beautifully-coloured seams. The Lantern Fish were very grateful for the redecoration, as it had needed doing for some time.

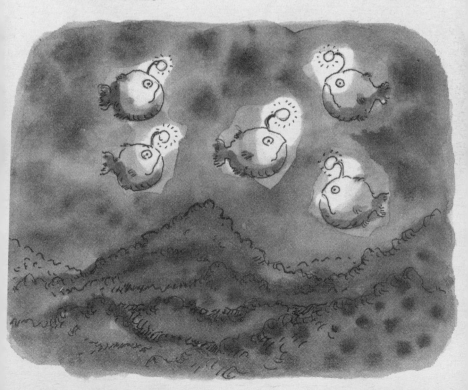

Next the Lantern Fish took up their positions on the seaweed ropes, faced in the same direction, braced their fins and heaved in unison, all their lanterns flashing as one. At first nothing happened. Then, bit by bit, the plug started to lift out of its hole and for the

first time in many years the oceans began to drain, the mountains to filter the sea and the rivers to flow with fresh sweet running water.

"Hold tight me hearties!" shouted Aunt Tabitha with excitement, for the current was sucking the bathysphere down the plug hole and the Lantern Fish were dashing for cover in their homes among the rocks.

"Stand by for more adventure!" she called, waving a packet of chocolate biscuits above the din. With incredible speed the bathysphere shot into the opening and down the tunnel.

Chapter 7

Timothy and his uncle and aunt buckled themselves in as the bathysphere sped along in the turbulent water. At first the tunnel was very wide and they couldn't see the sides, but it kept dividing to send branches to different parts of the world so that quite soon the tunnel wasn't much wider than the bathysphere itself.

The spotlights showed the walls rushing by so fast that they were a just a blur of weed, bubbles and stone.

"I wonder what will happen if we touch the tunnel sides," called Timothy to the others over the noise, his tennis-ball now dislodged on his head so that it was hanging over one ear.

Uncle Peregrine was about to shout a reply when they found out anyway. With a deafening clang the bathysphere hit the wall of the tunnel and bounced off again.

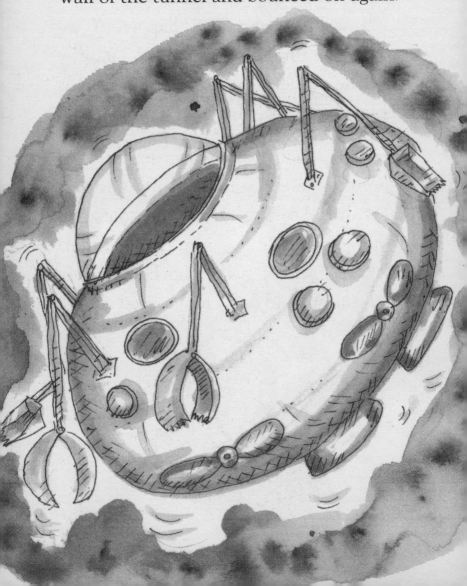

Aunt Tabitha and Uncle Peregrine looked at each other and grinned. No bathysphere had ever been so thoroughly tested. They unbuckled themselves and crawled around searching for leaks.

At the same time Timothy tried to see what had been lost from the outside. "One of the grabs has been ripped out at the roots and some of the lights have been smashed to bits," he shouted above the din.

No one had time to say or do anything else for they had to steady themselves against another grinding crash and a clang that seemed to ring in their heads over and over. They just had time to see the second grab disappear behind them before the remaining lights were squashed and everything went black outside.

"The batteries will be next," called Uncle Peregrine, and sure enough the instrument panel went dead as the next blow removed the batteries which were mounted on the bottom of the bathysphere for ballast.

Over and over they tumbled in the swirling inky blackness. Sandwiches, earrings, tennis-balls and marsupial skeletons all got mixed together as they journeyed at terrific speed through the insides of the earth.

After what seemed like hours of swirling and banging and scraping the noise suddenly stopped. Without knowing quite how, Timothy could sense that they had emerged into open water.

Looking upwards they could see a faint light which grew brighter and brighter as they rose towards it. All around them air bubbles glistened as they too found their way to the surface.

"It's tomorrow morning," whispered Timothy. "We've been under water all night."

Aunt Tabitha rubbed a porthole with her sleeve. "I wonder where we're going to come up," she said.

"It's just as well all those bits got knocked off," said Uncle Peregrine. "Otherwise we'd have been too heavy to surface and find out."

Eventually the battered and dented deep-sea bathysphere surfaced on a large and very beautiful lake in northern Siberia. After some busy paddling with the lid of the picnic hamper and a wooden spoon they made it to the

bank. There they rolled the faithful and terribly-dented bathysphere up the shore as best they could.

Pleased with the results of their expedition, and proud of the bathysphere, they sat down on the warm dry grass to rest. As the sun shone on their faces they sipped hot tea from a Thermos, ate chocolate biscuits and wondered what the Russian was for telephone.

The End